FEELING SPECIAL

Jennifer Kurani
illustrated by Valentina Jaskina

Sky Pony Press
New York

Turtle did not feel special.
He thought he was ordinary,
and that made him feel sad.
All his friends were special, though,
he thought.

Turtle went outside and saw Squirrel
running up and down a big tree.

He leaped from one branch to another branch very quickly! Turtle thought Squirrel was very special. Turtle was slow and could not climb trees the way Squirrel could.

Turtle felt ordinary and sad.

As he continued to walk, Turtle saw Bee
buzzing in a garden filled with colorful flowers.
Bee could fly! He had wings that helped him
fly from one flower to another flower. He was
gathering nectar to make sweet honey. Turtle
thought Bee was very special. Turtle could not
fly and make honey the way Bee could.

Turtle felt ordinary and sad.

He walked to the carrot patch and saw Rabbit hopping up and down. Rabbit could hop very high! His legs were so strong. Turtle thought Rabbit was very special. Turtle could not hop up and down the way Rabbit could.

Turtle still felt ordinary and sad.

Turtle wanted to feel special too!
What could make him special, he wondered?

Lost in his thoughts, Turtle did not realize how late it became. Soon the sky was dark, but he noticed a flickering light in the sky. It was Firefly!

He was flying too! Firefly could fly and light up the sky with his twinkling lights. Turtle thought Firefly was very special. Turtle could not fly or light up the sky.

Turtle felt ordinary and sad.

He slowly walked around and wondered
about how he could be special too.
He could not run fast or fly. He could not
hop up and down, or light up a sky.
Turtle did not feel special at all.

Soon it started to rain very hard and everyone was getting wet. Turtle quickly hid inside his hard shell to protect himself from the rain. He stayed dry and cozy inside the shell.

Suddenly, he realized that he was special too!
He had a hard shell to protect him
from getting wet in the rain.
He finally felt very special too!

Turtle realized that even though everyone is different, they are special in their own way. He no longer felt ordinary or sad.

Sky Pony Press books may be purchased in bulk at special discounts for sales promotion, corporate gifts, fund-raising, or educational purposes. Special editions can also be created to specifications. For details, contact the Special Sales Department, Sky Pony Press, 307 West 36th Street, 11th Floor, New York, NY 10018 or info@skyhorsepublishing.com.

Sky Pony® is a registered trademark of Skyhorse Publishing, Inc.®, a Delaware corporation.

Visit our website at www.skyponypress.com.

10 9 8 7 6 5 4 3 2 1

Manufactured in the United States of America, December 2018

This product conforms to CPSIA 2008

Library of Congress Cataloging-in-Publication Data is available on file.

Hardcover ISBN: 978-1-5107-4571-1
Ebook ISBN 978-1-5107-4572-8

Cover illustration by Valentina Jaskina
Cover design by Kate Gartner